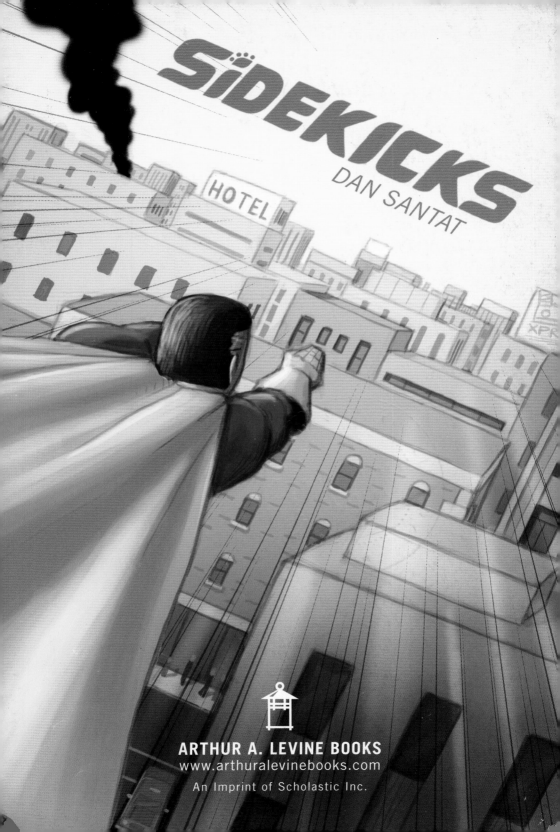

SIDEKICKS

DAN SANTAT

ARTHUR A. LEVINE BOOKS
www.arthuralevinebooks.com
An Imprint of Scholastic Inc.

TEXT AND ILLUSTRATIONS © 2011 BY DAN SANTAT

LIBRARY OF CONGRESS CATALOGING-IN-PUBLICATION DATA

SANTAT, DAN.
SIDEKICKS / WRITTEN AND ILLUSTRATED BY DAN SANTAT. -- 1ST ED.
P. CM.
ISBN 978-0-439-29811-7 (HARDCOVER)
ISBN 978-0-439-29819-3 (PAPERBACK)
1. GRAPHIC NOVELS. (1. GRAPHIC NOVELS. 2. SUPERHEROES--FICTION. 3. PETS--FICTION.)
I. TITLE.
PZ7.7.S17SI 2011
741.5'973--DC22

2010034704

10 9 8 7 6 5 4 3   11 12 13 14 15

BOOK DESIGN BY DAN SANTAT AND PHIL FALCO

FIRST EDITION, JULY 2011

PRINTED IN CHINA   95

FOR MY PARENTS.

−DAN SANTAT

THE NEXT EVENING...

ONE MORE THING— LET THE *SOCIETY OF SUPERHEROES* KNOW I'LL BE HOLDING SIDEKICK AUDITIONS NEXT MONTH. I COULD USE THEIR HELP.

YES, YOU HEARD RIGHT. I'M NOT GETTING ANY YOUNGER. IT'S TIME FOR ME TO GET SOME BACKUP AGAIN.

I'VE BEEN WORKING ON A DISGUISE IN CASE THIS EVER HAPPENED.

MOST SUPERHEROES DRESS LIKE ANIMALS ANYWAY. HE'LL JUST THINK I'M WEARING A FANCY DOG OUTFIT.

AND WHEN HE PICKS *ME*, I'LL GET TO SPEND MORE TIME WITH HIM WHILE *YOU* WATCH US ON THE NEWS.

WHAT MAKES YOU THINK I WON'T AUDITION TOO?

YOU? YOU DON'T HAVE A SUPERPOWER!

HEH HEH HEH

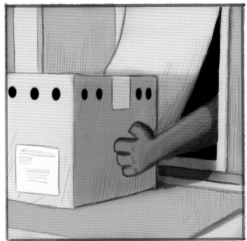

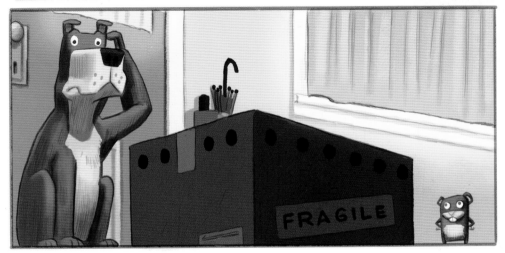

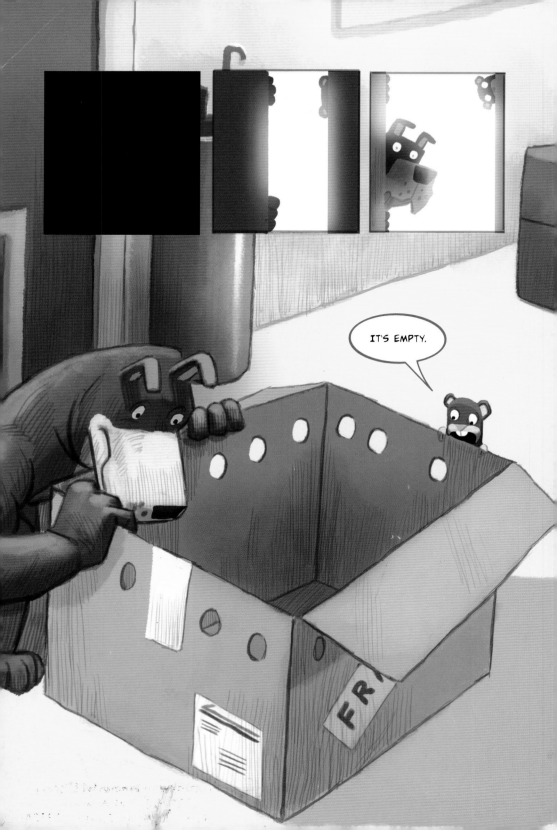

YOU MUST BE THE NEWEST MEMBER OF THE FAMILY!

BOYS, I FIGURED YOU COULD USE A NEW FRIEND AROUND HERE, SO I BOUGHT A CHAMELEON!

YOU'RE A SHIFTY-EYED LITTLE FELLA, AREN'T YOU?

I'LL CALL YOU *SHIFTY.*

YOU CAN BUNK WITH FLUFFY FOR NOW.

IS THAT OKAY, FLUFFY?

GOOD BOY.

:SIGH:

GURGLE

OH NO, NOT AGAIN!

GET ACQUAINTED, BOYS!

SLAM

WHERE AM I?

:SIGH:

YOU CAN SLEEP OVER IN THE OTHER CORNER.

OH... OKAY...

DON'T MIND ROSCOE; HE JUST NEEDS SOME TIME TO WARM UP.

OH, AND I'M FLUFFY. WELCOME TO THE FAMILY.

CITIZENS OF
METRO CITY,

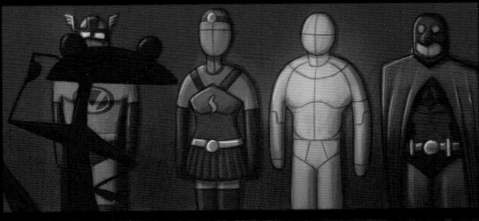

I AM PLEASED TO
ANNOUNCE THAT I HAVE BEEN
REFORMED BY OUR GREAT
JUDICIAL SYSTEM.

WHERE ARE
YOU GOING?

HUFFHUFFHUFFHUFF

WAIT!

36

I—I HAVE TO PEE.

UGH! I GUESS WE'LL START WITH THE BLUE ONE FIRST.

NO, NO, NO! I HAVE TO PEE *TOO!* I—

IT'S THE CLAW!!!

LET'S GET OUT OF HERE!

HEY, WAIT A SECOND. I THINK I KNOW THAT GUY.
ARE YOU NUTS!?!?!
PIZZA
STAY WHERE YOU ARE!
WHOA, WHOA, WAIT!

TOO OLD?

CRITICS ARE BEGINNING TO WONDER— IS CAPTAIN AMAZING GETTING *TOO OLD* TO DO THE JOB?

BEING OLD DOESN'T MAKE A PERSON WORTHLESS. HE'S STILL A VALUABLE ASSET TO METRO CITY.

CAPTAIN AMAZING IS OLD NEWS; WONDER MAN IS *MY* NEW HERO!

CLICK

58

STAY THERE AND DON'T MOVE.

HEY, BUDDY!

I'M NOT TOO KEEN ON PEANUTS AND I'D HATE TO SEE THEM GO TO WASTE. DO YOU WANT 'EM?

WHAT'S GOING ON HERE?! WHAT'S THE PROBLEM?!

RELAX, MUNGO, I WAS JUST GIVING MY STUDENTS HERE A LESSON IN CRIME FIGHTING.

WHEEZE WHEEZE WHEEZE

WHISPER
WHISPER
WHISPER . . .

AYE, AYE, SKIPPER!

HEY!

WHAT ARE YOU STILL DOING HERE?

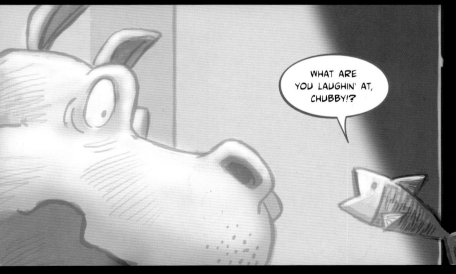

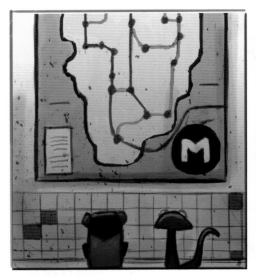

DID YOU HEAR THAT?!

HEAR WHAT?

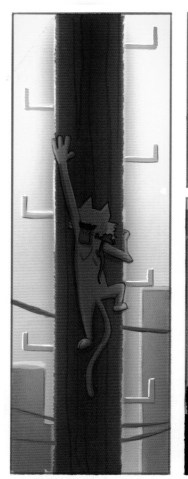

STAY HERE
WHILE I—
WAIT! WHO'S
THAT?!

KLANG!

8 DAYS LEFT...

WHUMP!

WHERE A—

WAIT HERE!

ξUGHξ

WHAT HAPPENED? WHAT DID WE HIT?

AAAH!

114

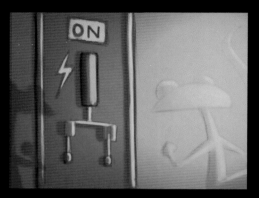

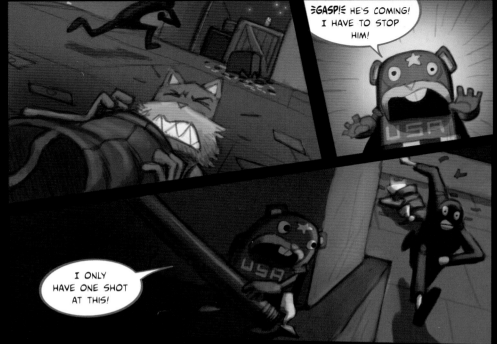

THANK YOU FOR YOUR HELP.

I'LL TAKE IT FROM HERE.

PLOP!

CLICK CLICK CLICK

FWOOSH!

SNIFF *SNIFF*

THAT GUY SMELLED FUNNY.... I...I CAN'T—

MANNY, YOU DON'T LOOK TOO HOT.

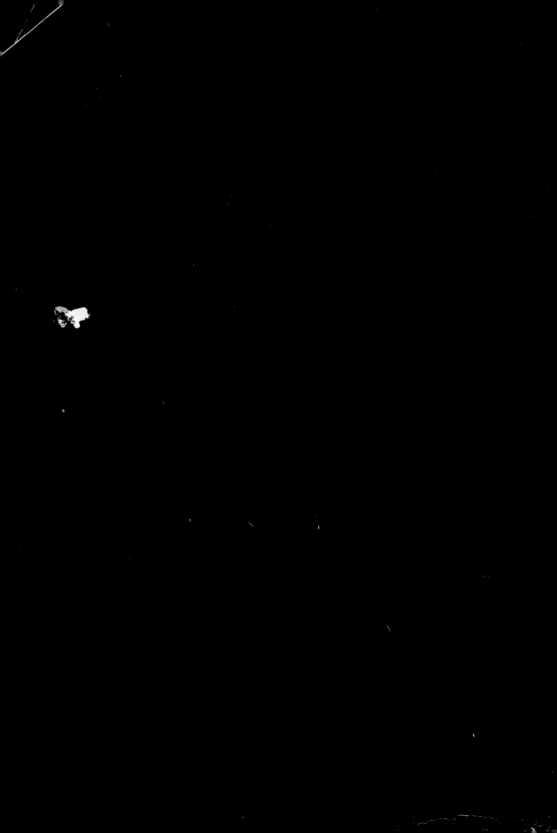

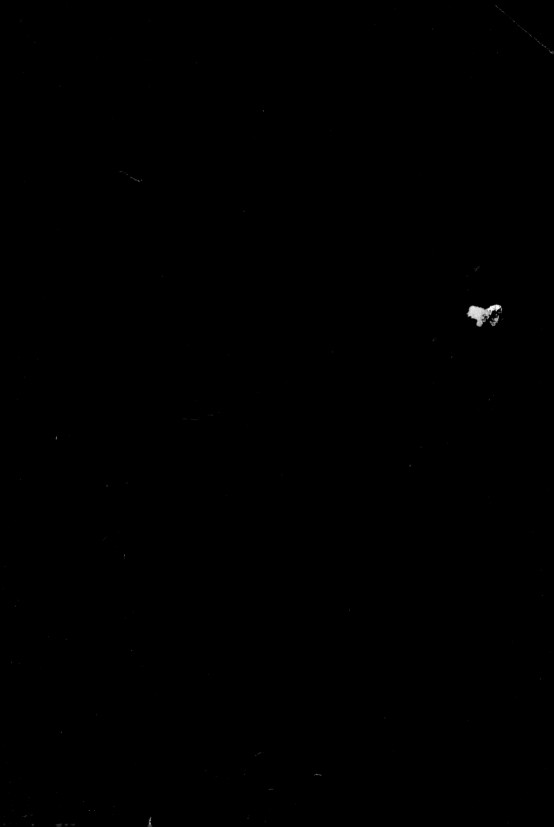

3 YEARS EARLIER...

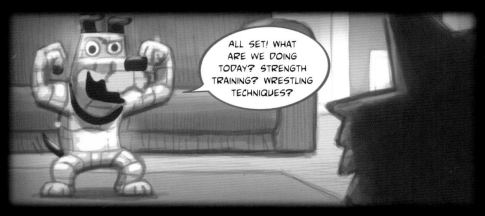

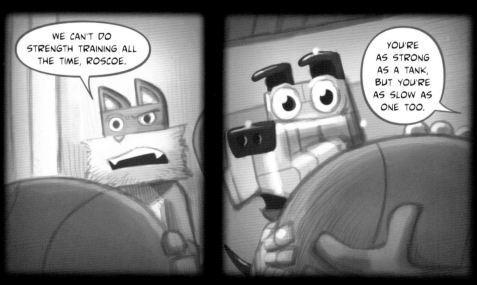

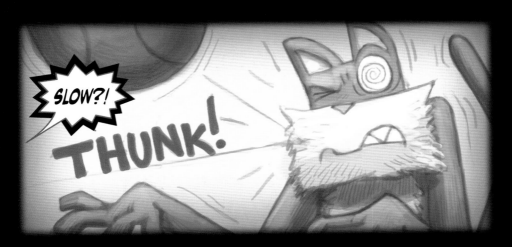

LEAVING SO SOON? A SIMPLE THANKS WOULD BE NICE.

WAIT, MANNY!

DON'T LISTEN TO ROSCOE. I KNOW I CAN DO THIS. I'VE LEARNED SO MUCH!

≡SIGH≡

WHY DO YOU WANT TO DO THIS, FLUFFY?

TELL ME THE TRUTH.

IT'S AN HONOR TO MEET YOU, CAPTAIN AMAZING.

HERE'S MY APPLICATION.

DON'T LOOK NOW, BUT WE MAY HAVE FOUND YOU A SIDEKICK.

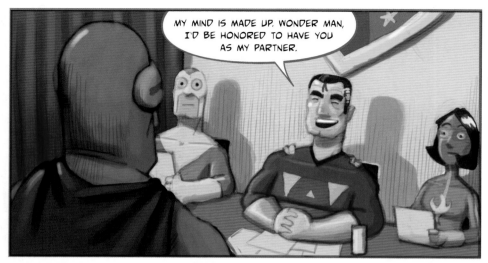

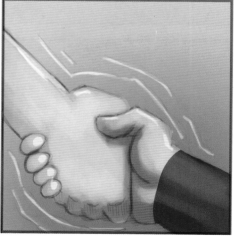

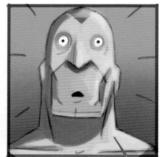

THE DNA TRANSFER DEVICE!

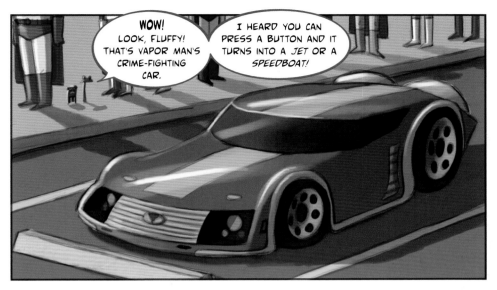

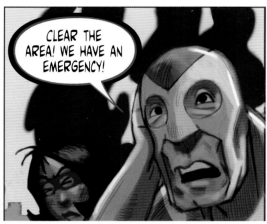

160

161

184

HE'S...

...GONE...

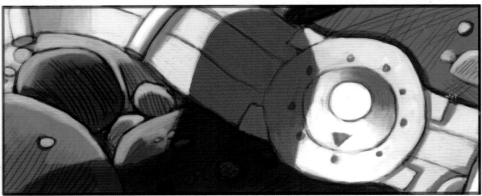

I'LL PROBABLY BE NEEDING THIS.

CAPTAIN AMAZING! WE'RE GLAD TO SEE THAT YOU'RE OKAY.

WE'LL HAVE A PRESS CONFERENCE ARRANGED FOR YOU IN TWENTY MINUTES.

THANK YOU, VAPOR MAN, BUT...NOT NOW.

WHAT?

IT'S TIME FOR ME TO GO HOME.

WOOSH!

APOLOGY ACCEPTED.

GZZZT!

THAT'S FOR BURYING NUMMERS!

OH, AND ONE MORE THING—

THANK YOU FOR SAVING MY LIFE.

YOU DID GOOD.

WELCOME BACK, FUR BALL!

THE END

SOCIETY OF SUPERHEROES
SIDEKICK APPLICATION

SIDEKICK POSITION FOR: CAPTAIN AMAZING

SIDEKICK NAME: WORKAHOLIC

(REAL) NAME: DAN SANTAT

AGE: 35   ADDRESS OF APPLICANT:

SEX: MALE   HEALTH INSURANCE PROV

CURRENT HERO RESIDENCE: LOS ANGELES

SUPER ABILITY: ABILITY TO FUNCTION
NORMALLY WITH LITTLE TO NO REST.

CONTACT INFO: WWW.DANTAT.COM

ARE YOU EVIL?:   Y   (N)

HAVE YOU EVER BEEN EVIL?:   Y   (N)

IF YOU ANSWERED "YES" PLEASE DESCRIBE

_____

_____

IS ANYONE IN YOUR FAMILY EVIL?: (Y)

IF YOU ANSWERED "YES" PLEASE DESCRIB
MY CAT HAS TENDENCIES TO
ATTACK MY WIFE WHILE ASLEEP.

_____

PLEASE PROVIDE A BRIEF BIO OF YOURSELF: DAN MADE HIS
PUBLISHING DEBUT IN 2004 WITH "THE GUILD OF GENIUSES."
SINCE THEN HE HAS GONE ON TO ILLUSTRATE MANY OTHER GREAT
TITLES SUCH AS "BOBBY VS. GIRLS (ACCIDENTALLY)" BY
LISA YEE, "OTTO UNDERCOVER" BY RHEA PERLMAN,
"CHICKEN DANCE" BY TAMMI SAUER, AND "OH NO! (OR HOW MY SCIENCE
PROJECT DESTROYED THE WORLD)" BY MAC BARNETT.   HE IS
ALSO THE CREATOR OF THE DISNEY ANIMATED
SERIES "THE REPLACEMENTS." THIS IS HIS SECOND BOOK.

ADDITIONAL INFORMATION: SUPER SPECIAL THANKS TO ARTHUR LEVINE,
RACHEL GRIFFITHS, DAVID SAYLOR, AND PHIL FALCO FOR HELPING ME
MAKE THIS BOOK SO SPECIAL (SEVEN LONG YEARS!). BIG SHOUT-OUT TO MY
SIDEKICKS CAMERON PETTY, MIKE BOLDT, JOHN GIBSON, TONY ETIENNE,
VINCE DORSE, AND OSKAR VAN VELDEN FOR COLORING ASSISTANCE,
AND LAST BUT NOT LEAST MY WIFE, LEAH, AND MY TWO KIDS. * HUGS! *

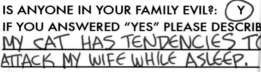

USE ONLY BLACK OR BLUE INK
PHOTO BY BRANDON KALPIN COPYRIGHT 2009